3

Well climb inside and make yourself comfortable. I'll unlock the door.

Right, if you're ready I'll begin.

THE STORY BEGINS AT THE SHOWROOM. I WAS BRAND NEW.

This is the one for us. We'll call him Clive.

THEN THERE WAS AN ADDITION TO THE FAMILY, ANDY.

SOON THERE WAS ANOTHER, SARAH.

IN NO TIME THEY WERE WALKING AND TALKING. THEY WOULD TALK TO ME AND I WOULD TALK BACK, AND TO MY SURPRISE THEY COULD HEAR ME.

Where are we going today, Clive?

Your Dad said we're going to the beach.

Were they surprised you could talk?

No, they grew up talking to me. It seemed normal.

What did Mum and Dad think?

They thought they were playing pretend games.

SOON WE WENT ALL AROUND THE COUNTRY.

That sounds such fun.

It was.

What was your favourite place?

THAT'S EASY. IT WAS A NICE SUNNY DAY ON THE BEACH. UP WOULD GO MY ROOF. MUM AND DAD WOULD COOK A MEAL ON MY COOKER. THE CHILDREN PLAYED ON THE SAND OR WENT SWIMMING.

We like the beach!

I can almost smell the sea and feel the breeze.

I wish we could go.

WE WENT TO THE BEACH A LOT. I SUPPOSE THAT WAS THE START OF MY PROBLEMS.

Problems, Clive?

Well, you know I'm made of metal.

Yes, steel.

AND STEEL REALLY DOES NOT LIKE SALTY WATER!

And there's lots of it at the beach.

Quite so, Jen.

THEN ONE DAY . . .

What's this? Looks like a bit of rust.

SOON MORE RUST WAS APPEARING.

There's rust around the window now.

Clive will be okay, won't he Dad?

Sure, his engine's fine. I'll just paint over the rust.

SO WE KEPT GOING JUST AS BEFORE, RUST AND ALL.

BUT THE RUST KEPT COMING BACK AND IN NEW PLACES.

So how did you end up here?

WELL, ONE TIME MUM AND DAD WANTED SOMEWHERE QUIET AND PEACEFUL.

SO WE CAME HERE. THERE WAS JUST A FIELD AND A TAP.

SARAH AND ANDY WERE EXCITED. THEY HAD NOT CAMPED ON A FARM BEFORE.

I NEEDED A BREAK AS WELL. OVER THE YEARS I HAD DRIVEN MANY THOUSANDS OF MILES. MY ENGINE WAS WEARING OUT.

COUGH! COUGH!

MY ENGINE WAS NOISY AND SMOKEY. I FELT REALLY EXHAUSTED.

ANYWAY, THE KIDS HAD A GREAT TIME EXPLORING THE FARM AND GOING FOR WALKS.

WHEN THE HOLIDAY WAS OVER AND IT WAS TIME TO GO, I REALLY TRIED BUT I COULD NOT START.

DAD GOT A MECHANIC OUT.

HE TINKERED WITH MY ENGINE, BUT HE COULDN'T START ME UP.

THE MECHANIC FROWNED.

Bad news. The engine's had it. You need a new one.

Is that expensive?

Yeah, really. It'll be about a couple of grand.

Andy and I can help you pay to mend Clive with our pocket money.

Even with your pocket money I don't think we can afford it.

And this camper is a rusty old thing. It'll fall apart soon, anyway.

What are you saying?

It's not worth spending more money on an old wreck like this.

FARMER JACK CAME OVER.

I've got an idea.

Leave your camper 'ere. I'll take it to the scrapyard.

THE SCRAPYARD!!

I HAD SEEN A SCRAPYARD BEFORE. IT WAS SCARY.

OLD CARS AND CAMPERS GO THERE. A HUGE CRANE GRABS THE VEHICLE WITH HIS CLAWS.

AND DROPS IT INTO A GIANT MASHER.

THE MONSTER MASHER CLOSES IT BIG JAWS AND CRUNCHES AND MUNCHES . . .

UNTIL ALL THAT IS LEFT IS A SMALL METAL CUBE.

I WAS SCARED AND SAD. I WAS LEAVING MY FAMILY. NEVER TO SEE THEM AGAIN.

I suppose I have no choice, but I can't tell the kids.

Just tell them I'm keeping the camper to do it up.

Good idea!

Yeah.
Now phone for a taxi. I'll speak to the little 'uns.

Hey, Kids come 'ere!

What is it Farmer Jack, can you help?

Your Dad says I can keep your camper and do it up.

That's great!

Thank you Farmer Jack. It's so nice to know he will have a lovely new home.

We can come and see him when he's done up.

You'll be so happy together. You're so kind Farmer Jack.

So this is where I have been ever since.

There you are. Well, what have you found here?

He's really special!

We could keep him and do him up!

Huh. Nice idea, but I just don't have the time, kids.

We can help you, Dad. It'll be fun.

Hey, aren't you forgetting something? This camper belongs to Farmer Jack.

He belonged to a family like yours, and I'd love to see 'im done up. Tell you what, you 'ave 'im.

What? But . . .

You've got the trailer – take 'im.

Please?

Hmm, it could make a nice camper.

Oh, please, Dad.

Look, I'll get him back to the workshop and just have a look.

HOORAY!

Bye Ol' Fella. Enjoy your new home.

What's on your mind, Dad?

Just what am I going to say to your mum.

Oh, the kitchen.

That's right. I promised to start the kitchen this weekend.

I'm sure when Mum meets Clive she won't mind, cos he's special.

13

Well, it's just that I'm scared

Scared? What of?

Tomorrow I'm taken completely apart!

I see what you mean. I would be scared if that happened to me.

And when that happens I shall go away for a while.

Like being asleep?

Yes, Danny, a bit.

But you'll be back once Dad puts you together again?

That's what scares me the most. You might have a shiny new camper but. . .

It might not be you Clive.

I might just be an **ordinary** camper.

One that doesn't talk.

That's right.

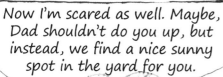
Now I'm scared as well. Maybe, Dad shouldn't do you up, but instead, we find a nice sunny spot in the yard for you.

Yes, but eventually I would get so rusty I would collapse into a pile of metal dust.

And then you would be gone.

It would not be for a while and not so scary, but . . .

But, what?

We would not have the adventures I planned. If your Dad can get me back on the road we'll have such fun.

Clive, my Dad's the best mechanic ever. And we'll make sure he saves as many of your parts as he can.

And put them back in exactly the right place.

Yeah, you'll be alright, Clive.

But in the end, Clive, it's your decision.

Thanks, you've both been a great help, and now I have made up my mind. With you kids looking out for me I can get through this.

So Dad can renovate you?

He sure can!

Oh, Clive, that's fantastic.

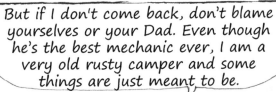
But if I don't come back, don't blame yourselves or your Dad. Even though he's the best mechanic ever, I am a very old rusty camper and some things are just meant to be.

Right, you had better say good night now, because we have a busy time tomorrow.

Okay, Goodnight, Clive.

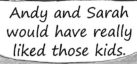
Andy and Sarah would have really liked those kids.

THE NEXT DAY

Right, let's take the interior out first.

Okay Dad, but you have to give us all the bits to look after.

We'll make sure everything goes back exactly as it should.

That's fine by me. Give them a good clean as well.

We could get Mum to help us.

Huh, that won't happen. Mum's not too keen on this project.

What with me not getting the kitchen done for a while.

Leave it to us, we know how to win her round.

Mum, we've got this stuff to clean that Dad has taken out of Clive.

Don't look at me, I'm far too busy.

That's okay Mum, we're going to do it.

Yes, can we have the scouring pads? Some of the cabinets are really dirty.

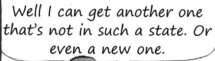
Well I can get another one that's not in such a state. Or even a new one.

But Dear, they've got their heart set on this one. You can't stop now.

I thought you'd be pleased. I can get on with the kitchen.

Oh sure.

No, I really will get started on it. I promise.

Look is fixing the camper completely impossible?

Well, it's tricky. There's heaps of rust to cut out and loads of welding.

It could be done, but it'll take forever.

Hmm, forever, eh? So no longer than the kitchen then?

Alright, don't rub it in. But why the change of mind?

Come with me, I'll show you

Look at this.

It's parts from Clive, all cleaned and numbered.

Yes, it all has been identified down to the smallest bolts. They know where it all goes.

If they can put all this effort in to this, then Clive obviously means a lot to them.

You know they think it can talk.

Yes, they're just using their imagination that's all.

So what's it to be, carry on or give up?

Well, if you put it like that, carry on I suppose.

Good. If you've finished your tea, I suggest you'd better get back to it.

What? Oh yes Dear.

Did you hear that? Mum persuaded Dad not to give up.

That's Clive for you, he makes friends with everyone.

Look at this, children. I've found an old photo that had fallen behind the camper drawers.

That must be Andy and Sarah.

They are right. How on earth did they know that?

Did Clive tell them? That's ridiculous isn't it?

Clive, talk to us.

He's gone, Danny. Just like he said he might. He's never coming back.

Don't get upset children. I'm sure your Dad can do something.

I don't know what I can do! I can't see what's wrong with it.

We need to wake him up somehow.

How? He is in such a deep sleep, he can't hear us.

Does he have a favourite song we could sing? That might do the trick.

I don't know Mum, he never said.

Is there something else that he really likes?

Think Danny, what did Clive say his favourite things were?

Hmmm, what did he say? Sun, sand castles, surf . . .

THE BEACH! He loves the beach!

We need to get Clive to the beach.

But how? We can't drive him there he won't start.

But Dear, Clive told them his favourite place is the beach. It's worth a try.

Clive TOLD them?

I know. I'm not really sure what is going on . . .

but there is something special about this camper. He's unique.

What does unique mean?

It means there is only one Clive the Classic Camper.

Hi Kids! What's going on?

Clive! You're back!

Dad restored you. You're really smart.

Look at this photo we've taken of you.

Is that me? Wow!

Tell you're Dad he really is the world's best mechanic.

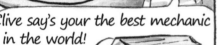

Clive say's your the best mechanic in the world!

Thank you Clive. Now can the World's Best Mechanic have something to eat? I'm famished.

Well I think we should eat outside . Your head is too big to fit inside Clive.

Can someone take a photo of me cooking in the camper?

Why is that Mum?

The photo is to remind me how cramped it is in there, if I ever think of coming again!

But Dear, I thought we could go camping next weekend.

And another time we could go to France.

THE END

✻ Colour me in ✻

CLIVE THE CLASSIC CAMPER / ILLUSTRATION: CHRIS STAPLE

Design your own paint job for Clive

Here's a tip: draw the design in pencil before colouring it in.

CLV 1

CLIVE THE CLASSIC CAMPER / ILLUSTRATION: CHRIS STAPLE

Printed in Poland
by Amazon Fulfillment
Poland Sp. z o.o., Wrocław